W9-AVZ-316

CHARLES DICKENS

DISCARD

E CIN
Cinar, Lisa, 1980-
The day it all blew away /
413305   DI

The Day It All Blew Away

By Lisa Cinar

FOR ALL THE AWESOME KIDS AT CHARLES DICKENS

For my Mom and Nan

First published in 2007 by Simply Read Books Inc.
www.simplyreadbooks.com

Text & illustrations copyright © 2007 Lisa Cinar

All rights reserved. No part of this publication may be
reproduced, stored in a retrieval system or transmitted, in any
form or by any means, electronic, mechanic, photocopying, recording
or otherwise, without the written permission of
the publisher.

We gratefully acknowledge the support of the Canada Council
for the Arts and the BC Arts Council for our publishing program.

Library and Archives Canada Cataloguing in Publication
Cinar, Lisa, 1980-
      The day it all blew away / Lisa Cinar.
ISBN 978-1-894965-71-2
      I. Title.
PS8653D39 2007   jC813'.6   C2007-9001454-2

Printed in Singapore

10 9 8 7 6 5 4 3 2 1

Design by Steedman Design

The Day It All Blew Away

By Lisa Cinar

Simply Read Books

Part One

Some time ago, there was a person,
and his name was Mr. Tadaa.

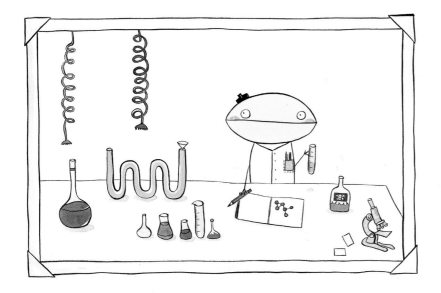

*Mr. Tadaa liked to go to social
events and to 'educational' places,
as well as on long walks.*

But Mr. Tadaa had a problem. His head was very big,
and MUCH too huge for his tiny hat.

This was very much of an inconvenience, since you see, every time Mr. Tadaa would become acquainted with new people the hat thing would become a horrible nightmare! The new acquaintances would tip their hats and look at Mr. Tadaa. Now it was Mr. Tadaa's turn to tip his hat...

... but because Mr. Tadaa's head was so big, it was very hard for him to locate his hat, and so it took him a long,

loong,

looooooooooooooooooooooong,

time to find his hat, in order to tip it, and be...

polite.

And Mr. Tadaa was polite! Oh very!
No question about it!

But it's hard to be polite all the time.

Oh, grasshoppers
and fiddlesticks

*Especially if it takes you one or two hours to find your hat
so you can tip it.*

Not only did this make it hard for Mr. Tadaa to meet people, but he also felt left out many times. He even had the occasional feeling that he was being made fun of.

One day, as Mr. Tadaa went on one of his walks, a sudden a gust of wind...

blew his hat away.

Naturally, Mr. Tadaa ran after it.

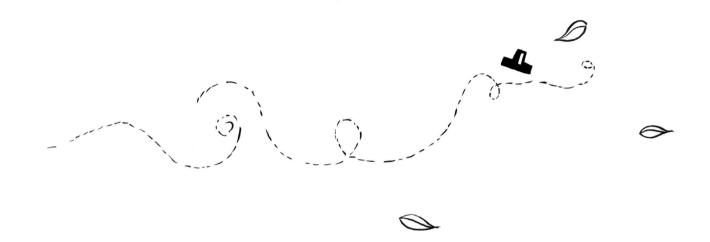

Part Two

Some time ago, there was a hat, and his name was Ahh.

Ahh was unnaturally large for his occupation, and since his person
was MUCH smaller than Ahh, he simply carried the person around on
top of him, making things easier for them both.

When people would see the little person who belonged to the hat, they would tip their hats and say, "Hello, little person."

Then the little person would scream: "Tip, Ahh, Tip!" And then the hat would tip,

but of course the little person would fall to the ground.

This simple routine was quite tedious for everyone!

One rainy day, they went for a walk.
Ahh loved it, but the little person was less excited.

All of a sudden, along came a gust of wind, and off flew the little person!

Naturally, Ahh the hat ran after it.

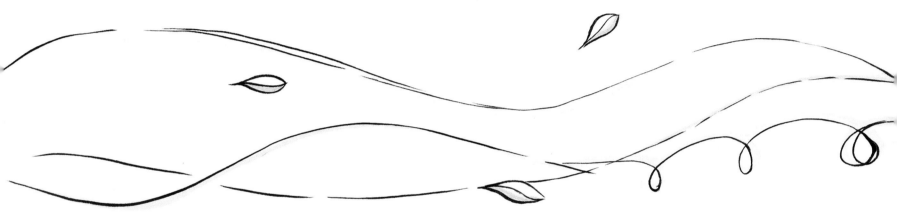

As Ahh chased after the little person and Tadaa
chased after his little hat, a funny thing happened.

Because the big hat was so proud that he could run so fast, and to show the little person that he had arrived, he yelled: "TADAAAAA!"

And because Tadaa was so surprised to see a huge top hat that was yelling his very own name, he screamed, "AHHHHH!"

Now I know what you might think would have happened. Mr. Tadaa took Ahh as his hat, and the little person was content with Mr. Tadaa's old hat, and they lived happily ever after...

But it wasn't so. It was not so.

Because the hat Ahh was actually much too big for even Mr. Tadaa's mountain of a head,

and since the little person was not used to wearing a hat, they both found wearing the new hats quite uncomfortable and unnecessary.

What DID happen, though... was that all of them became very good friends.

*And they **ALMOST** never made fun of each other.*

Together they would go to social events, like the Great Soda Party held in honour of the arrival of Prince Tipperton,

The 10th Annual Outdoor Fall Dance Tournament,

or the famous Hopple Hobble Sack races.

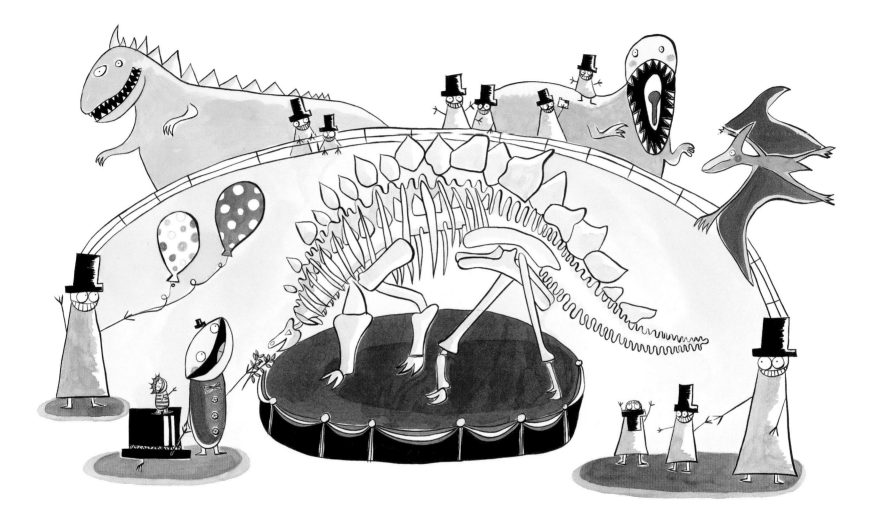

Even the educational places that Mr. Tadaa was so very fond of, like the Amazing Dinosaur Museum,

and the Museum of Children's Art *(which, of course, only accepts art by children, and not from silly adults).*

They also went on hiking trips, to which Mr. Tadaa always brought his wildlife book and taught them many names of plants, insects and animals.

Now when people would tip hats to them they would simply smile very nicely instead. At times however there would be some hat tippers who just couldn't tolerate that the friends wouldn't tip their hats to them. Even when they all gave their best smiles and greeted them in the friendliest way possible.

When this happened, Mr Tadaa, the little person and the hat Ahh just couldn't stand it any longer. They would look at the hat tipper and scream at the top of their lungs: "Tip, Ahhhhhh, Tip!" This would shock and confuse the frustrated hat tipper, but the friends thought it was hilarious!

And then they would fall down laughing, until their faces were all stretched out and their stomachs hurt.

And when it was Mr. Tadaa's birthday, Ahh and the little person both chipped in and got him a big umbrella.